Shortcut on the Oregon Trail

SRA

Columbus, OH

SRAonline.com

 SRA

Send all inquiries to this address:
SRA/McGraw-Hill
4400 Easton Commons
Columbus, OH 43219

ISBN: 978-0-07-608773-0
MHID: 0-07-608773-5

2 3 4 5 6 7 8 9 NOR 13 12 11 10 09

Emily had been walking since dawn through the endless prairie. How many hours? Ten? Twelve? Emily and her parents were heading west on the Oregon Trail with thirty other families. They walked so the oxen would not have to pull both their weight and the weight of all their belongings.

They had left their home in Illinois where Emily's father worked as a farmhand. In the West they would homestead the land and have their own farm. They had brought only their cow, clothes, a dresser, food, and a cast-iron pot.

Her mother called, "Can you make it a bit farther?"

Before she could answer, Emily's father said, "Sure she can. She's tough."

Emily sighed and stumbled on, leading the family cow by an old rope. The cow didn't look any happier than she did about the trek.

"We can cut off about five days from our trip if we take the shortcut," she heard her father say. "That's nearly eighty-five miles."

Her mother replied, "But there's no water on that route!"

"It will be a challenge, but people have done it. If we take Sublette's Cutoff we will get there almost a week earlier."

"If we get there at all," Emily's mother said. "We have been traveling for four months, and we are all alive and safe. We could get lost if we leave the main trail. Then what will happen to us, especially without water?"

Emily pretended not to hear. What would happen if they were stranded so far from anyone else?

"We'll stop here for the night," her father said, ignoring Emily's mother's question. He heaved the big black pot out from the back of the wagon.

"Tell me again about our new home, Ma," Emily said as she helped prepare dinner.

"We'll have 640 acres of farmland," her mother said.

"It's free for homesteaders like us, right?" Emily said. Her mother nodded.

"We can grow corn and wheat as tall as trees, I'll bet!" Emily said.

As they talked, the men pitched the tents made from raggedy sheets. They ate bacon, beans, and dried fruit. Emily went to sleep early because her feet were sore and her head hurt. She lay still, thinking about their new life in the West. Then she heard her father whispering to her mother.

"We are running low on supplies," he said, "so I've made a decision. We will take Sublette's Cutoff." Her mother didn't answer. "We'll ask around. Maybe other families will come too."

In the morning Emily's father spoke to other men in the camp about the shortcut.

"There's very little grass for our cattle and oxen to eat on that trail," one of the men told her father, "and I hear there's no water for almost fifty miles."

Emily swallowed hard. No water.

"But it will save us nearly a week of traveling," her father said.

The men turned to their wives and talked. Six families finally agreed that taking the shortcut was a good decision.

Seven wagons lined up, and the procession began.

"Spread out!" Emily's father called to the wagon drivers.

The wagons took their positions in wide rows to start the long trek. If they rode too close to each other, everyone would be coughing and rubbing their eyes from the dust raised by the rolling wheels.

Emily walked next to her mother while her father guided the oxen.

The air was dry, and there was no grass—just barren land.

"Empty the wagons!" her father directed. They started the long process of unloading the two thousand pounds of supplies so the wagons could safely go down the hill. The women led the unhitched animals.

"We'll take them one at a time," her father said.

The men gathered around the first wagon. They held tight to the back and gently eased the enormous wagon slowly down the hill. The men groaned as they kept the heavy wagon from flipping. Then it was time for the next wagon and the next.

Emily's family's wagon was the last one. When the men pushed it to the edge, the wagon jerked forward and slid beyond the men's grip. They scrambled desperately to reach it but could not get to it in time.

The rickety wagon crashed to the bottom of the hill, and one of the wheels broke.

"We'll fix it," Emily's father said.

"There's no water around," said one of the men. "We can't waste a whole day here trying to fix it. We've spent too much time already."

Another man agreed, saying, "Put your things in our wagons."

"I cannot abandon my wagon," Emily's father said.

He rummaged through his tools, and another man helped him. The others wiped their sweaty foreheads and waited under the burning sun.

Emily's scalp was sweaty and itchy under her bonnet. She was so thirsty and could see the others were too.

The man who was helping said, "I don't think we can fix it. Maybe we'd better get your belongings into our wagons instead."

Her father answered, "I have another wheel."

All the men heaved the heavy wagon up, and Emily's father pulled on the broken piece of wheel. Finally he yanked it loose from the axle, which was broken too.

"You can't fix that!" one man said.

"What about using an ax handle or two?" Emily asked, her throat scratchy with thirst. "You can use a rope to lash them to the axle to keep it straight and strong."

"That would make the axle strong enough for a while," her father said.

The wheel was wobbly, but after some of the heavier supplies were moved to other wagons, it was good enough.

Fixing the wheel and reloading the supplies had taken two days. Now with the sun at its hottest, they began their journey again.

Emily dragged her feet over the dry land with her parents. The oxen and the cow stumbled on. There were no trees offering shade, no breeze, and no water. Emily saw some wagon wheels littering the barren land.

Days passed, and still they walked. Then one day Emily saw the end of the tall prairie grass and the dry land. She saw beautiful green countryside with ponds and yellow and purple wildflowers!

The group had walked almost two thousand miles, and Emily knew she was home. She and her parents had made it across the Oregon Trail. Now a better life filled with new adventures and great prosperity could begin!

Vocabulary

prairie (prâ´ rē) (page 3) *n.* A large area of level or rolling land with grass and few or no trees.

trek (trek) (page 4) *n.* A long, slow journey.

challenge (chal´ ənj) (page 5) *n.* A call to take part in a difficult task or contest.

pitched (pitchd) (page 7) *v.* Past tense of **pitch**: To set up.

raggedy (rag´ i dē) (page 7) *adj.* Torn or worn out.

procession (prə sesh´ ən) (page 9) *n.* A group of persons moving forward in a line or in a certain order.

desperately (des´ pə rət lē) (page 11) *adv.* Hopelessly.

rickety (ri´ ki tē) (page 11) *adj.* Likely to fall or break; shaky.

Comprehension Focus: Visualizing

1. Visualize yourself walking the Oregon Trail on a very hot day. Write a paragraph about what you see, hear, touch, feel, and taste.
2. Reread the descriptions of the two routes in the story. Draw a picture of how you visualize one of them.